Zara
the Starlight Fairy

by Daisy Meadows

ORCHARD

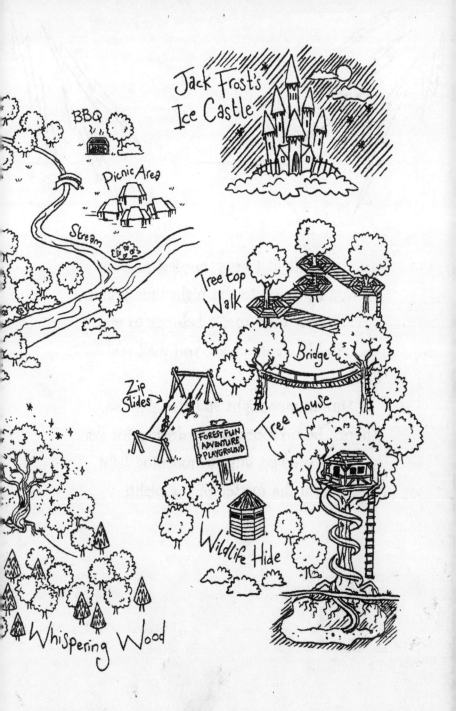

The Twilight Fairies' magical powers
Bring harmony to the night-time hours.
But now their magic belongs to me,
And I'll cause chaos, you shall see!

Sunset, moonlight and starlight too,
There'll be no more sweet dreams for you,
From evening dusk to morning light
I am the master of the night!

Contents

Contents

A Star is Born!

"This telescope is huge, Kirsty!" Rachel Walker said excitedly to her best friend, Kirsty Tate. "I can't wait to have a look at the night sky."

"It's going to be amazing," Kirsty agreed as they stared up at the enormous silver telescope.

The girls were spending a week of the

summer holidays with their parents at Camp Stargaze, which had its very own observatory for studying the stars. The observatory was a square white building topped with a large dome, and charts and pictures of the night sky hung on the walls. In the middle of the observatory stood the gigantic telescope, and Professor Hetty, the camp astronomer, was explaining to Rachel, Kirsty and the other children about the stars and constellations.

"As you know, this area was chosen for Camp Stargaze because we can get really clear views of the night sky from here," Professor Hetty reminded them. She was a jolly, round-faced woman with twinkling blue eyes and a mop of red hair.

"Have any of you ever done a join-the-dots puzzle?"

Everyone nodded.

"Well, a constellation is rather like a join-the-dots puzzle!" Professor Hetty explained with a smile. "A constellation is made of individual stars that join up to make a picture, just like the puzzle. But although the stars look close together to us here on earth, sometimes they're actually millions of miles apart! Let's take a look, shall we?"

Professor Hetty pressed a button on the wall. There was a noise overhead,

and Rachel and Kirsty glanced up to see
a large section of the domed roof slide
smoothly back. This revealed the dark,
velvety night sky and sparkling silver stars
twinkling here and there like diamonds
in a jewellery box. Everyone gasped
and applauded.

"Wonderful!"
Professor
Hetty said
eagerly.
"I never get
tired of looking
at the night sky.
It's so magical."

Rachel nudged Kirsty.
"Professor Hetty doesn't know just
how magical the night-time really is!"
she whispered.

Kirsty smiled. When she and Rachel had arrived at Camp Stargaze, Ava the Sunset Fairy had rushed from Fairyland to ask for their help. The girls had discovered that Ava and the other six Twilight Fairies made sure the hours from dusk to dawn were peaceful and happy, with the help of their satin bags of magical fairy dust.

But while the Twilight Fairies were enjoying a party under the stars with their fairy friends, Jack Frost had broken into the Fairyland Palace with his naughty goblin servants. The goblins had stolen the magical bags that were hidden under the Twilight Fairies' pillows. Then, with a wave of his ice wand, Jack Frost had sent the goblins and the bags spinning away from Fairyland to hide in the human world. Jack Frost's plan was to cause night-time chaos for both fairies and humans, but Rachel, Kirsty and the Twilight Fairies were determined not to let that happen.

"I wonder if we'll meet another Twilight Fairy today?" Kirsty murmured to Rachel as they all lined up to have a look through the telescope. "I'm so glad we managed to find Ava's and Lexi's magical bags, but we still have five more to go!"

"Remember, we have to let the magic come to us," Rachel reminded her.

The girls' new friend, Alex, was first to use the telescope, and Professor Hetty showed her how to look through the eyepiece. Alex peered into the telescope eagerly.

"Everything looks so close!" she gasped.

"Can you see any pictures in the stars,

Alex?" asked Professor Hetty.

"I think I see something…" Alex peered more closely. "Oh!" She burst out laughing. "I can see a constellation shaped like a toothbrush!"

"Well done," said Professor Hetty. "And those of you who aren't  using the telescope should be able to see it too, if you look hard."

Rachel and Kirsty gazed intently up at the sky.

"Oh, there it is!" Kirsty exclaimed, pointing out the toothbrush of stars to Rachel. "And it even has bristles!"

"Lucas, it's your turn," Professor Hetty said.

Lucas, another of Rachel and Kirsty's friends, took Alex's place at the telescope. He studied the sky for a few minutes and then turned to Professor Hetty.

"That constellation near the toothbrush looks like a pair of pyjamas," he said with a grin.

"Right again!" Professor Hetty smiled. "Did you spot the slipper constellation too, just below the pyjamas, Lucas?"

Lucas looked again. "Yes, I can see it now," he said. "It really is like a join-the-dots puzzle!"

It was Rachel's turn after Lucas had finished.

"I'll just change the angle of the

16

telescope a little, Rachel," Professor Hetty told her. "Then you should be able to spot something different."

Rachel peered through the glass eyepiece. At first she got a shock because the stars looked so close and were so bright. Then, as her eyesight adjusted, she saw the constellation shaped like a slipper that Professor Hetty had mentioned earlier.

"This is amazing!" Rachel gasped.

"Can you see any other constellations, Rachel?" Professor Hetty asked.

Rachel stared at the night sky. For a moment she couldn't see anything new, and then all of a sudden she noticed that some of the stars seemed to be grouped together in the outline of a face. The face had spiky hair and a spiky beard as well as a pointy nose.

"I think I see a face," Rachel said hesitantly.

"A face?" Professor Hetty sounded very surprised. "I wasn't expecting that!" And she gazed up at the night sky, trying to spot it for herself. Meanwhile, Rachel was frowning. That face in the stars looked familiar...

"Aha, I see it now!" Professor Hetty exclaimed. "And look, everyone – a star has drifted away from the toothbrush constellation to join up with the face. We're actually seeing a new constellation forming in front of our very eyes. How amazing! I've never seen anything like it!"

"Kirsty, look at this!" Rachel said quickly, moving aside to let her friend take her place at the telescope.

Kirsty took a good look at the

constellation as the drifting star settled into its new place, becoming part of the face's spiky beard. Her eyes widened as she realised exactly who it was.

It was Jack Frost!

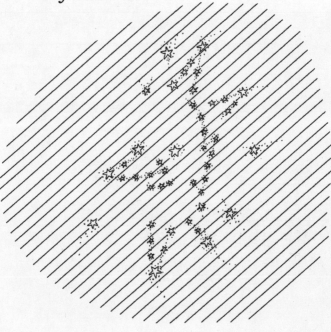

Zara Zooms In

"Surely Jack Frost's face can't be a real constellation?" Kirsty murmured to Rachel as they followed Professor Hetty and the others out of the observatory.

"Well, Professor Hetty seems to think it is!" Rachel replied. The professor was so excited by the new constellation that she hadn't stopped talking about it. "But we know that Jack Frost must be using the Twilight Fairies' magic to create havoc in the night sky."

Outside the observatory Peter, one of the camp leaders, was waiting to introduce the evening activity. Immediately Professor Hetty began telling him about the new constellation.

"And look, Peter, some stars are moving across from the other constellations to join it!" she explained.

Rachel and Kirsty glanced upwards. Several more stars had detached themselves from the pyjamas constellation that Lucas had spotted earlier, and were floating across the sky. As the girls watched, the stars positioned themselves on Jack Frost's face, forming his familiar, icy grin.

"Right, everyone, we're going to do some orienteering this evening," Peter told them.

There was a murmur of excitement.

"Oh, great," said Kirsty. "We did orienteering when we stayed at that adventure camp, didn't we, Rachel?"

Rachel nodded. "It's fun," she agreed. "And it'll give us a chance to look around and try to find out what Jack Frost is up to!" she added in a low voice.

"First, get into pairs, and I'll give you a map of the constellations and a compass,"

Peter went on. "You should use them to find three locations within the camp, and each location name is the clue to a puzzle. Then, when you get to the last location, there's a surprise waiting!"

"But you'll have to be quick," Professor Hetty called as she and Peter began handing out the compasses and maps. "This is a great night to be out under the stars because we can watch this new constellation forming. But if you take too long, more stars will have moved, and you may not be able to find your way!"

Kirsty looked up at the night sky again. The outline of Jack Frost now had a neck and the beginning of shoulders.

"At this rate there won't be any constellations left in the sky except Jack Frost!" she told Rachel.

Rachel looked dismayed. "That would be awful!" she exclaimed, as her eye was caught by another sparkling star floating across the dark sky.

But this time the star didn't join the Jack Frost constellation. Instead it suddenly plunged down towards the earth, leaving a trail of golden sparks behind it like a firework. Rachel clutched Kirsty's arm.

"Kirsty, I think that might be a shooting star!" she gasped.

As the two girls watched, the star spiralled downwards and disappeared behind the observatory. No one else had noticed because they were too busy studying their maps.

25

Kirsty and Rachel slipped away quietly
and ran to the observatory, their hearts
thumping with excitement.

"Girls," called a clear, tinkling voice,
"I'm over here!" And suddenly a tiny fairy
popped out from behind the observatory.

"It's Zara the Starlight Fairy!" Rachel
said.

"Hello, Zara," said Kirsty. "Welcome
to Camp Stargaze!"

Zara smiled as the girls rushed over
to her. She wore an oversized T-shirt
scattered with stars,
black leggings and
silver shoes, as
well as a silver
star bracelet
and matching
necklace.

"Yes, it's me, girls," she replied. "And I'm sure you've noticed that Jack Frost is using my magical star dust to move all the stars around?"

Kirsty and Rachel nodded.

"Jack Frost is so vain, he wants a big picture of himself in the sky every single night!" Zara explained.

"So he's stealing stars and ruining all the beautiful constellations. That means ships won't be able to navigate at sea, and birds which fly at night and use the stars to find their way will get lost, too. It'll be chaos! My bag of star dust is around here somewhere, so will you help me find it and stop Jack Frost?"

"Of course we will!" Rachel and Kirsty cried.

Scattered Star Dust

"Thank you, girls," Zara said gratefully.

"We can look for your bag of star dust while we search for the three mystery locations," Rachel pointed out, switching on her torch and shining it onto the map.

"To find the first location, go north, and mind you don't slip!" Kirsty read out. She placed the compass on the map and the three friends watched the needle swing around and point north.

"Mind you don't slip…" Rachel repeated thoughtfully, looking up at the stars. "Oh! I think that means the first place we have to find is right underneath the slipper constellation. That's north from where we're standing."

"Luckily, the slipper still has most of its stars, so let's go right away," Zara suggested.

Quickly Zara flew down to perch on Kirsty's shoulder, hiding behind her hair. Then the girls set off towards the slipper constellation. The other children, including Alex and Lucas, were still studying their maps, staring at the stars and trying to work out how to use the compass. But then Rachel noticed two boys wearing baggy T-shirts, shorts and baseball caps also heading off in the direction of the slipper constellation. They barged rudely past Alex and Lucas, knocking the map from Lucas's hand.

"Hey, watch out!" Lucas called. But the two boys didn't stop.

"Looks like those boys have worked out where the first location is, too," Rachel remarked as she and Kirsty made their way through the tents.

Suddenly, there was the sound of twittering overhead. Surprised, Rachel and Kirsty glanced up and saw a flock of beautiful, bright blue birds flying above them.

The birds were tweeting miserably,
turning their heads as if they were
searching for something.
"Oh no!" Zara
gasped, popping
out from behind
Kirsty's hair. "This
is exactly what
I told you would
happen, girls. These birds
are Blue Buntings and they fly at night,
using the stars to find their way. They're
completely lost!"

"Poor things," said Kirsty as the birds
flew on, still chirping sadly to each other.
"We must find your bag of magical dust
and put the stars back in the right place,
Zara."

Zara nodded. "We're almost right

underneath the slipper constellation now, girls," she pointed out.

Rachel was shining her torch just ahead of them. "I can see something between the tents!" she said. "It's a signpost and it has a number '1' on it."

"Well done, girls!" Zara exclaimed. "You've found the first location. And just in time, too…"

Rachel and Kirsty looked up at the slipper constellation, and saw several more stars slide away to make up the outline of one of Jack Frost's arms.

"I hope everyone else manages to find it too," Kirsty said anxiously. "There's hardly any of the slipper left now."

"There's something glowing at the bottom of the signpost," Rachel said. "I wonder what it is?"

"We saw it first!" yelled a voice behind them.

Zara rushed to hide again as two boys ran out of the shadows and pushed roughly past them. Rachel recognised them as the same boys who'd barged Alex and Lucas out of the way earlier.

"Look, prizes!" one of them shouted gleefully. "And they're all for US!"

Rachel and Kirsty could see now that there was a pile of glow-in-the-dark star stickers heaped at the bottom of the signpost.

"You shouldn't take them all," Rachel called as the two boys grabbed the stickers. "I think they're meant for everyone."

The boys ignored her and began sticking the stars all over themselves.

Then, shrieking with glee, they ran off.

"That wasn't very nice of them, was it?" Kirsty sighed as the two boys, glowing all over with stars, disappeared from sight again. "What's the next clue, Rachel?"

Rachel looked at the map again. "To find the second location, go west and brush up on your orienteering skills!" she read out.

"West is that way," Kirsty said, staring down at the compass. "And I guess the clue means that we have to look underneath the toothbrush constellation!" She peered up at the sky and frowned. "But where is it?"

"It's vanished!" Rachel gasped. "Look, Jack Frost has got both his arms now. He must have stolen all the stars from the toothbrush constellation."

"Not quite," Zara chimed in. "I know the usual positions of the stars so well that

I can see there's still one bit of the toothbrush left. Look at that lone star just there." And Zara pointed her wand at a single star twinkling away on its own. "That's what's left of the toothbrush constellation."

Just then the girls heard footsteps behind them, and Zara quickly whisked out of sight.

"Hi, you two," Kirsty called as a glum-looking Alex and Lucas came towards them. "How are you getting on?"

"Not very well," Lucas sighed. "We were trying to make our way to the first location underneath the slipper constellation, but so many of the stars have moved that now we're lost."

"You're heading in the right direction," Rachel told them, pointing towards the first signpost.

"Thanks!" Lucas and Alex looked more cheerful and dashed off.

"Let's hurry, Rachel," Kirsty said anxiously, "before all the toothbrush disappears!"

Fixing their eyes on the single star, the girls headed to the west of the campsite. As they went, they met several other children

who were lost and confused because of
the shifting stars, and Rachel and Kirsty
helpfully directed them to the first location.

But as the girls went on their way, using
their torches to light up the darkness,
Kirsty suddenly tripped over something.
She gasped, staggered and almost fell.

"Kirsty, are you OK?" cried Zara, flying
off her shoulder.

"I'm fine," Kirsty replied. She shone her
torch downwards and saw that the laces
on one of her trainers had come undone.
Kirsty bent to retie it, but then, to her
surprise, she noticed tiny pinpricks of glitter
on the ground. "Zara, Rachel, look at
this!" she called.

Zara swooped down to see. "That's my
star dust!" she exclaimed. "But how did it
get there?"

Rachel moved her own torch slowly across the ground, picking out the specks of fairy dust. "I think they've been trodden into the ground by someone," she declared. "See those big, clumsy footprints?"

"Goblin footprints!" Kirsty gasped. "Those two rude little boys must be goblins in disguise! They're the only ones who are ahead of us."

"And they've got my bag of star dust!" Zara added.

Glow-in-the-dark Goblins!

"Well, at least they've left us a trail of star dust to follow to the second location!" Rachel said with a grin. In the torchlight, the three friends could see the star dust sparkling into the distance. "Off we go!"

The trail of glittering fairy dust led Zara and the girls through the campsite and towards the entrance to Camp Stargaze.

"I think the second location must be near the gate to the camp," Kirsty said. "Look, it's right underneath the only star left of the toothbrush constellation."

"You're right, Kirsty," Rachel added, directing the beam of her torch at the camp entrance. "I can see a signpost with '2' on it. There's a big silver foil star pinned on the gate, too."

"And there are the glow-in-the-dark goblins!" Zara whispered.

The goblins, still covered in stickers, were kneeling on the ground under the signpost.

They were greedily scooping up handfuls of star-shaped chocolates and shoving them into their pockets.

"More prizes!" yelled the biggest goblin, who had glowing stars stuck on each ear like giant earrings.

"Stop that!" Kirsty called. "Those chocolates are for everyone!"

The smaller goblin, who had a star sticker on the end of his long, pointy green nose, scowled at her.

"Go and find your own prizes!" he shouted, grabbing the last few chocolates. Then both goblins jumped up and raced off into the dark Whispering Wood. Dazzling specks drifted around them, leaving a trail of fairy dust through the trees.

"I'll turn you into fairies, girls," Zara said. "Then we can chase after the goblins quickly, and without being seen." She fluttered above the girls' heads, showering them with fairy magic from her wand. Instantly Rachel and Kirsty shrank down to the same size as Zara with delicate, glittery wings on their backs.

"There go the goblins!" Zara called as they saw two glowing figures dart between the trees. "We can follow them easily, even in the dark, because of those star stickers they're wearing. Come on!"

Zara, Rachel and Kirsty zoomed into the Whispering Wood. For a moment they couldn't see the goblins at all, but then Kirsty spotted a faint glow through the undergrowth.

"There they are!" she whispered.

The goblins were running along one of the paths in the wood. Zara and the girls followed them at a safe distance, swerving neatly around the trees and keeping well out of sight. At last the goblins skidded to a halt beside a tall oak tree. Immediately Zara, Rachel and Kirsty landed on a branch just above their heads and hid among the leaves.

"I think we've got away from that pesky fairy and her silly friends at last!" the biggest goblin panted. "Let's eat our chocolate."

Zara and the girls watched as the goblins sat down under the tree and began to empty their pockets, heaping the chocolate stars on the grass. Then they saw the biggest goblin take out a shiny satin bag and throw it on top of the pile of chocolates.

"It's my bag of star dust!" Zara whispered.

The goblins unwrapped some of the chocolate and scoffed it greedily.

"Jack Frost is going to be very pleased with his constellation," the smallest goblin said smugly.

He opened Zara's bag and tossed a
handful of magical
dust onto the
grass, where it
sparkled like
tiny jewels.
"Maybe he'll
give us another
prize!"

The biggest goblin didn't answer
because he was cramming another
chocolate star into his mouth. Just then
Zara and the girls saw one of the Blue
Bunting birds flying towards them.

Rachel and Kirsty were amazed by how
big the bird was now that they were
fairy-sized. Looking rather forlorn, the
Blue Bunting landed on the same branch
where the three friends were perched.

"This poor bird must be lost," Zara whispered.

Suddenly the bird fluttered off the branch again and swooped down to the ground, skimming right over the top of the goblins' heads. They shrieked with fear.

"What's that?" the biggest goblin wailed through a mouthful of chocolate.

"It must be a pogwurzel!" the other goblin yelled, shivering and shaking all over. "Let's get out of this scary dark wood!"

Quickly the biggest goblin grabbed
the bag of star dust and the remaining
chocolates and then they both took to
their heels. Zara, Rachel and Kirsty flew
after them, but then
Rachel noticed the
light of a torch
ahead of
them.

"Someone's
coming!" she
whispered
to Zara and
Kirsty, and
the three of them
ducked behind a bush.

A moment later, Peter came down
the path and bumped right into the two
goblins.

"Aha, so you're the boys who've stolen all the prizes!" Peter said crossly, spotting the chocolates the biggest goblin was carrying. Rachel, Kirsty and Zara breathed a sigh of relief when they realised that, although Peter had a torch, the goblins' faces were hidden in the shadows.

"That's very greedy. Give them back, please." And he held out his hands.

"My bag of star dust is right in the middle of that pile of chocolates!" Zara said anxiously. "We can't let the goblins hand it over to Peter."

"Don't worry," Rachel replied, "I have an idea. Quick, Zara, make me and Kirsty human-size again!"

Scary Shadows

Immediately Zara swished her wand and Kirsty and Rachel shot back up to their normal size in a cloud of fairy dust.

"Hello, Peter," Rachel called, running out from behind the bush. Kirsty followed, wondering what Rachel's plan was. "We found those chocolates in the woods," Rachel went on, "and these boys are helping us to carry them back to the signpost by the gate."

"Yes, that's exactly what we're doing!" the smallest goblin chimed in quickly.

"Oh, so it wasn't you who took them," Peter said to the goblins. "Sorry about that. OK, make sure you put them back so that the others can find them." And with a smile, he went off. Kirsty and Rachel heaved sighs of relief.

"We just helped you, so now you can help us," Rachel told the goblins. "Give us the bag of star dust, please." She pointed up at the sky where the Jack Frost constellation now had legs. "It's time the

stars were back in their proper place."

"And you can go and put the chocolates back, too," Kirsty added.

The goblins glanced at each other. "You must be joking!" the smallest goblin yelled. He grabbed some of the chocolates from the other goblin and began throwing them at the girls. The biggest goblin joined in, pelting Rachel and Kirsty so hard with chocolates that they were forced to run back towards the bush to escape.

"Stop it!" Zara shouted, flying out from behind the bush to see what was going on.

Having used up all the chocolates, the goblins turned and dashed off. The biggest goblin was still clutching the bag of star dust tightly.

"After them, girls!" called Zara, waving her wand around Rachel and Kirsty.

When the girls were fairy-sized again, they all zoomed after the two goblins. They were running along one of the paths that led back to Camp Stargaze.

"We won't be able to chase the goblins through the camp," Rachel pointed out, dismayed. "Someone might see."

"Maybe we should keep them here in the Whispering Wood," Kirsty suggested. "They're nervous because it's dark and scary."

"You're right, Kirsty," Zara agreed. "It might be our best chance of getting my bag away from them. Let's chase the goblins back among the trees!"

The three friends linked hands and flew very fast so that they could get in front of the goblins. Then they swooped down, hovering in front of them and blocking their path.

"It's those fairies again!" the biggest goblin shouted, spinning around. "Quick, run the other way!" And the two goblins charged back into the thickest part of the wood.

"Quickly, girls!" Zara whispered.

Rachel, Kirsty and Zara whizzed around
the goblins, herding them deeper into
the wood. Whenever one of the goblins
tried to take a path that led back to the
campsite, Zara and the girls would zoom
down and block their way.

"But how are we going to get the bag
of star dust back?" Kirsty panted as she
flew around the goblins' heads. "We need
a plan!"

All of a sudden, though, Kirsty's heart

began to pound with
fright. A great
black shadow
was flying
through the
darkness,
heading

straight towards her. Quickly she swerved
out of its way, but when it
came closer she was
very relieved to
see that it was
only one of the
Blue Bunting
birds fluttering

through the trees. It had looked very
dark and scary with its giant wings and
enormous beak.

"Oh!" Kirsty exclaimed, flying over to
Rachel and Zara. "I think I know how
we can get the bag of star dust back from
the goblins!" She took her fairy-sized torch
out of her pocket. "Look…"

Kirsty switched the torch on and pointed
the beam at Zara. Instantly a gigantic
shadow with enormous wings and long

arms and legs appeared on the broad
trunk of a tree behind her.

"Look!" the biggest goblin shouted,
pointing at the shadow looming over
them. "What's that?"

Rachel grinned. She flew into the
torchlight too, and a
second enormous
shadow sprang up
next to Zara's.

"There's
another!"
the small
goblin
yelped.

With a
quick flick
of her wand
Zara spun a

cloud of magical fairy dust around herself
and the girls.

"WE'RE WATCHING YOU!" Zara
called to the goblins. But her spell had
changed her sweet, silvery voice to a loud,
scary roar.

"YOU SHOULDN'T
HAVE STOLEN ALL
THE PRIZES!"
said Rachel, trying
not to laugh as
her voice, now
as loud and
frightening as
Zara's, boomed
through the
tree. "THAT
WAS VERY
NAUGHTY!"

"They must be pogwurzels!" the big goblin wailed, terrified.

"And they're not just pogwurzels," moaned the small goblin. "They're giant pogwurzels! Help!"

Rachel switched her torch on too, and she, Kirsty and Zara took turns at swooping around in front of the beams of light, casting their huge shadows all over the trees around them. The goblins moaned with fear and clung to each other, their knees knocking together.

"DROP THE BAG OF STAR DUST AND WE'LL LET YOU GO!" Kirsty roared in her pogwurzel voice.

Would the goblins give in and return Zara's bag?

Starry Party

The goblins stared at each other in a panic.

"What shall we do?" groaned the big goblin. "Jack Frost will be really angry if his constellation disappears!"

"Do you want to get eaten by pogwurzels instead?" the small goblin demanded. "Which is worse – Jack Frost or pogwurzels?"

The big goblin hesitated for a moment. Then he yelled "Pogwurzels!" Quickly he hurled the bag high in the air towards the giant shadows, and then he and his friend dashed off through the trees.

Smiling, Zara zoomed over and tapped the bag with her wand. It immediately shrank down to fairy-size and Zara caught it as it fell.

"We did it, girls!" Zara declared happily. "Now everything in the night sky will soon be back to normal. Let's go and see."

Rachel and Kirsty followed Zara as she flew upwards through the trees.

Then they hovered above the
Whispering Wood, staring at the sky. The
stars were already sliding away from Jack
Frost's arms and legs and back to their
own constellations. As the girls watched,
Jack Frost gradually got smaller and
smaller until only his icy grin was left.
Soon, even that was gone.

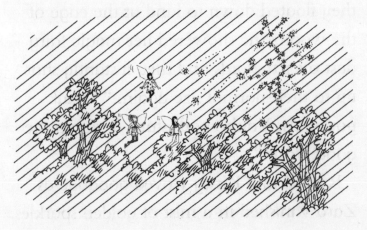

"All the stars are back in the right
place," Rachel sighed happily. "The night
sky looks beautiful."

"And the birds can find their way again," Kirsty added as the flock of Blue Buntings swooped past them calling happily to each other.

"I must give everyone in Fairyland the good news," Zara said as they floated down to land at the edge of the wood. She showered her magic fairy dust over the girls and they instantly shot up to their normal size again. "Thank you, girls. You're both stars! Keep up the good work!"

Rachel and Kirsty waved goodbye as Zara vanished in a mist of golden sparkles.

"Look, the pyjamas constellation is the only one on the map left to find now, and it's right above the observatory," Rachel pointed out as they went back to camp.

"And there's the third signpost outside the observatory door," said Kirsty. "This is the last location."

All the other children, including Alex and Lucas, were also heading to the observatory.

"Now that the stars are back in their proper places, they can follow their maps!" Kirsty whispered to Rachel as Peter gathered everyone round.

"Well done!" Peter said. "Can anyone put the three locations together and solve the puzzle?"

Everyone started talking, trying to work it out.

"The first location was in the camp among the tents," Kirsty murmured to Rachel.

"The second was the gate with the silver star on it," said Rachel.

"And the third was the observatory," Kirsty added. "And we gaze at the stars from the observatory, so it must be—"

"CAMP STARGAZE!" the girls called together.

"You've got it!" Peter said, and everyone applauded. "Now, come into the observatory. Professor Hetty and I have a surprise for you."

Everyone crowded into the observatory where Professor Hetty was waiting for them. The walls were decorated with glow-in-the-dark stars and there was a table laid with sandwiches and cakes.

"It's a starry party!" Professor Hetty laughed, handing out glasses of squash. "It's been fun watching the strange events in the sky, but I'm glad everything's back to normal."

As the party got underway, Rachel and Kirsty sneaked a peek through the giant telescope.

"There's Zara!" Kirsty whispered, pointing to a golden light floating in the sky.

As the girls watched, the golden light burst into a shower of sparkles. Then the sparkles formed themselves into a dazzling constellation in the shape of a fairy. It hung there glittering in the sky for a few moments, and then disappeared.

Rachel and Kirsty glanced at each in delight. It was a wonderful ending to yet another thrilling fairy adventure!

Now Kirsty and Rachel
must help...

Morgan the Midnight Fairy

Read on for a sneak peek...

"I'm not tired at all, are you?" Kirsty Tate asked her best friend Rachel Walker. It was late at night and the two girls were in the Whispering Wood, shining their torches into the shadows as they collected firewood. They were staying with their families at a holiday centre called Camp Stargaze, and tonight the whole camp were having a midnight feast together.

"Not a bit," Rachel replied, tugging at a branch from the undergrowth. "I'm way too excited to even think about being tired!" She grinned at Kirsty. "What a brilliant holiday this is turning out to be. A whole week together, lots of adventures, a midnight feast and…" She lowered her voice, glancing around cautiously. "And plenty of fairy magic too!"

Kirsty smiled. It was true – she and Rachel had been having a wonderful time so far this week.

On their very first evening in camp, they'd met Ava the Sunset Fairy, who was one of seven Twilight Fairies. The Twilight Fairies looked after the world between dusk and dawn, making sure that everything was as it should be with the help of their special bags of magical dust. But a few nights ago, naughty Jack Frost had stolen these bags while the seven fairies were having a party together.

Kirsty and Rachel were friends with

the fairies and had had lots of exciting adventures with them before, so when the Twilight Fairies asked if they would help search for the stolen fairy dust, Kirsty and Rachel were happy to say yes.

So far they had found three bags of magic dust belonging to Ava the Sunset Fairy, Lexi the Firefly Fairy and Zara the Starlight Fairy, but there were still four left to find.

Read Morgan the Midnight Fairy to find out what adventures are in store for Kirsty and Rachel!

Meet the
Twilight Fairies

**Kirsty and Rachel must rescue the Twilight
Fairies' magical bags from Jack Frost or
nobody will ever enjoy a night's rest again!**

www.rainbowmagicbooks.co.uk

Meet the fairies, play games
and get sneak peeks at
the latest books!

www.rainbowmagicbooks.co.uk

There's fairy fun for everyone on
our wonderful website.
You'll find great activities, competitions, stories and
fairy profiles, and also a special newsletter.

Get 30% off all Rainbow Magic books at

www.rainbowmagicbooks.co.uk

Enter the code RAINBOW at the checkout.
Offer ends 31 December 2012.

Offer valid in United Kingdom and Republic of Ireland only.

Win Rainbow Magic Goodies!

There are lots of Rainbow Magic fairies, and we want to know which one is your favourite! Send us a picture of her and tell us in thirty words why she is your favourite and why you like Rainbow Magic books. Each month we will put the entries into a draw and select one winner to receive a Rainbow Magic Sparkly T-shirt and Goody Bag!

Send your entry on a postcard to Rainbow Magic Competition, Orchard Books, 338 Euston Road, London NW1 3BH.
Australian readers should email: childrens.books@hachette.com.au
New Zealand readers should write to Rainbow Magic Competition, 4 Whetu Place, Mairangi Bay, Auckland NZ.
Don't forget to include your name and address.
Only one entry per child.

Good luck!

Meet the
Showtime Fairies

**Collect them all to find out how Kirsty and
Rachel help their magical friends to save
the Tippington Variety Show!**

www.rainbowmagicbooks.co.uk